For
Liz Wood and David Lloyd

First U.S. edition 2012

Library of Congress Cataloging-in-Publication Data is available.

Library of Congress Catalog Card Number pending

ISBN 978-0-7636-5867-0

11 12 13 14 15 16 SCP 10 9 8 7 6 5 4 3 2 1

Printed in Humen, Dongguan, China

This book was typeset in Historical Fell Type.
The illustrations were done in mixed media.

Candlewick Press
99 Dover Street
Somerville, Massachusetts 02144

visit us at www.candlewick.com

Arthur's DREAM BOAT

Polly Dunbar

CANDLEWICK PRESS

One night Arthur
had a dream.

It was amazing.

"Wow!" Arthur said to his dog.

"Last night I had a dream."

"It was amazing," Arthur told his brother. "Last night I dreamed about a pink-and-green boat with a striped mast."

TIPPETY-
TAP,
TIPPETY-
TAP.

"Mom," Arthur called. "Last night I dreamed about a boat. It was pink and green with a striped mast and polka-dotted sails."

"Hey!" shouted Arthur to his sister.

"Last night I dreamed about a boat.

It was pink and green

with a striped mast

and polka-dotted sails—

and it had a golden flag."

SPLITTER,
SPLATTER,
SPLASH!

"Dad!" cried Arthur.

"Last night I had a dream.

It was about a pink-and-green

boat with a striped mast,

polka-dotted sails,

a golden flag, and

a beautiful figurehead."

But nobody was listening.

"**LISTEN TO ME!**

I'm *trying* to tell you

about my . . .

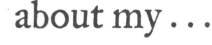

REAM BOAT!"

SSSHHH

SSSHHH SSSHHH

"Ahoy!"

"Arthur!"

"ALL
ABOARD!"

One night Arthur

had a dream.

And it really was . . .

amazing!

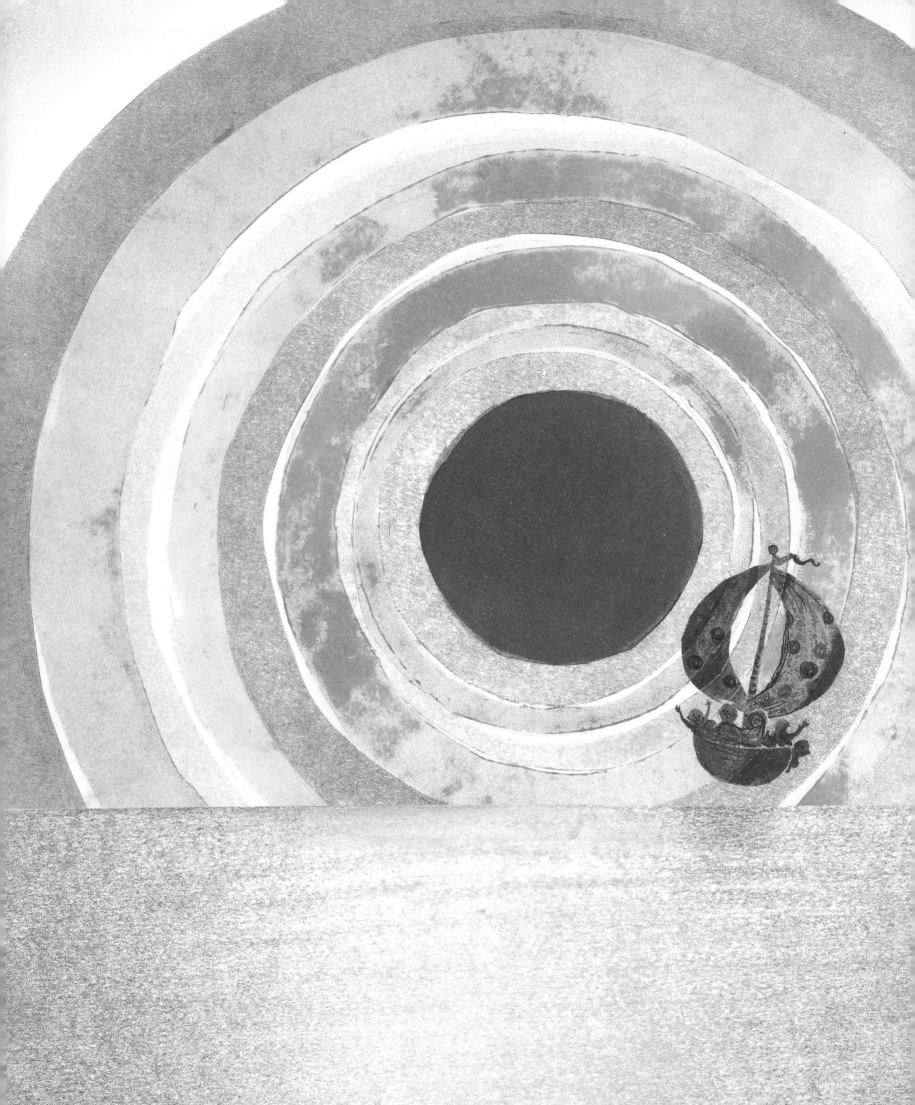